For Sienna
SG

For Lone
LG

Reading Consultant: Prue Goodwin,
lecturer in education at the University of Reading

ORCHARD BOOKS
338 Euston Road, London NW1 3BH
Orchard Books Australia
Level 17/207 Kent Street, Sydney, NSW 2000
ISBN 978 1 84362 402 8 (hardback)
ISBN 978 1 84362 405 9 (paperback)
First published in hardback in Great Britain in 2007
First paperback publication in 2008
Poppy and Max characters © Lindsey Gardiner 2001
Text © Sally Grindley 2007
Illustrations © Lindsey Gardiner 2007
The rights of Sally Grindley to be identified as the author and
of Lindsey Gardiner to be identified as the illustrator of this work
have been asserted by them in accordance with the
Copyright, Designs and Patents Act, 1988.
A CIP catalogue record for this book is available from the British Library.
1 3 5 7 9 10 8 6 4 2 (hardback)
1 3 5 7 9 10 8 6 4 2 (paperback)
Printed in Hong Kong
Orchard Books is a division of Hachette Children's Books,
an Hachette Livre UK company
www.orchardbooks.co.uk

Poppy and Max and the Sore Paw

Sally Grindley ❧ Lindsey Gardiner

ORCHARD BOOKS

One sunny day, Poppy and
Max were feeding the ducks in the
park, when they saw their friends
playing football.

"Come and play with us," called Jack and Sam.
"Brilliant!" cried Poppy.
"I love football."

"Bags I go in goal," said Max.
They used Poppy's bag and Sam's
jumper to mark out the goal.

Max stood ready.
Poppy and Jack and Sam took turns
to shoot.

Max leapt to the left, he leapt to the right, he leapt high in the air, and he saved every ball.

"Great goalkeeping, Max," said Poppy.
"Nobody can beat Max when he's in
goal," boasted Max.

"I bet I can beat you," boasted Jack.
"I bet you can't," said Max.

Jack took the ball and placed it in front of the goal. Then he walked away from it, turned round and ran up to it as fast as he could.

POW! He kicked the ball with all
his might.
"Save it, Max!" yelled Poppy.

Max leapt high, high in the air and caught the ball. As he landed, he yelped loudly and let go of it.

It trickled slowly behind him, over the line between Poppy's bag and Sam's jumper.

"Goal!" shouted Jack and Sam.

"Paw!" howled Max. He rolled around on the ground.

"What's the matter, Max?" asked
Poppy.
"I've hurt my paw," whimpered Max.
"Poor Max," said Poppy.

"Can you walk?" asked Jack.

"Oooo, no," whimpered Max.

"It's too sore."

"We'll have to carry him," said Sam.

They picked him up and took a few steps, then they put him down with a bump.

"Ouch!" squealed Max. "I've got a sore bottom *and* a sore paw now."
"You're too heavy, Max," puffed Poppy.

"Let's put him in that wheelbarrow there," said Jack.
"Brilliant idea!" cried Poppy.

"I am not a dog who likes being put in a wheelbarrow," sniffed Max.

"Pretend it's a pram," said Poppy.
"I am not a baby!" grumbled Max.
"It's the wheelbarrow or walk," said Sam.

They lifted Max into the wheelbarrow.
BUMP, BUMP, BUMP, they wheeled it
down the path.

"OUCH, OUCH, OUCH!" moaned
Max. "I'll have a sore paw and a sore
bottom and a sore head if you're not
more careful."

"Poor Max," said Poppy.
As soon as they were home, Jack
and Sam lifted Max on to a chair.

Poppy began to wrap a bandage round Max's paw.

"Eeeek!" squealed Max. "Not too tight."

"When this is done," said Poppy, "I'll make you a nice mug of hot chocolate."

"And muffins," said Max. "A dog with a sore paw needs muffins."
"And muffins," agreed Poppy.

"And a hot water bottle," said Max.
"A dog with a sore paw needs a hot
water bottle."
"And a hot water bottle," agreed Poppy.

"I'm beginning to feel better already," said Max.

Poppy and Jack and Sam looked at each other and grinned.

"It's not such a bad injury then,"
said Jack.

"Oh it is," said Max. "Very bad. But
I don't like to complain. I'm a very
brave dog, you see."

"Yes, you are," smiled Poppy.
"Very brave indeed."

Sally Grindley
Illustrated by Lindsey Gardine

Poppy and Max are available from all good bookshops,
or can be ordered direct from the publisher:
Orchard Books, PO BOX 29, Douglas IM99 1BQ
Credit card orders please telephone 01624 836000 or fax 01624 837033
or e-mail: bookshop@enterprise.net for details.

To order please quote title, author and ISBN and your full name and address.
Cheques and postal orders should be made payable to 'Bookpost plc'.
Postage and packing is FREE within the UK
(overseas customers should add £1.00 per book).

Prices and availability are subject to change.